D1368753

The GOOSE on the ROOF

Written by Sarah Sommer

Illustrations by Martina Terzi

To anyone who's ever had a conversation with an animal.

There's a goose on my roof, and he won't go away.
He's been honking all night and all through the day.

There's a goose on my roof, and he won't come down.
Won't somebody please help me stop this sound?

I'm just so tired of the squawking all the time,
but what should I do? The goose isn't mine!

There's a knock on the door—the neighbor's complaining:
"Keep it down, please. I have guests I'm entertaining!"

"I'm sorry," I said, and I promised I'd go
talk to that goose about his honking show.

So I ran outside and found a frog who said,
he could leap really high to the shingles overhead.

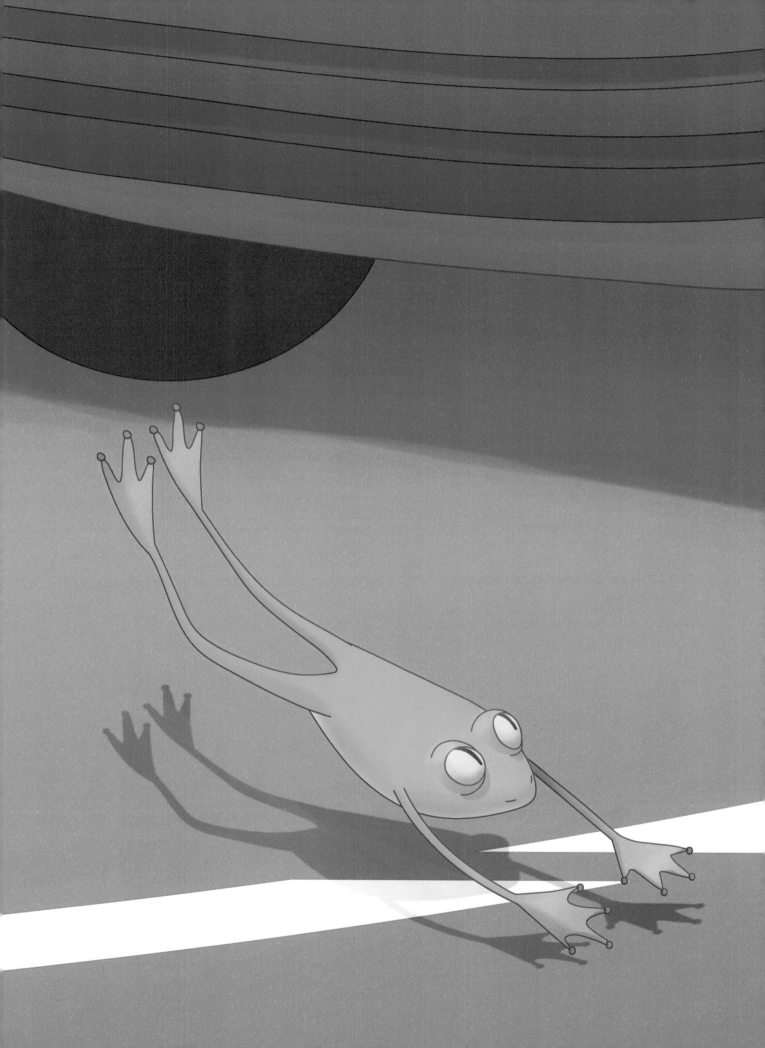

But he jumped too far in the wrong direction,
and now he's trapped in a busy intersection.

Then I asked for a hand from a nearby cat
who claimed she could chase away the goose like a rat.

But the cat soon froze halfway up the tree,
and now she's too scared to come back down to me.

Then out of the sky came a blue butterfly
who offered to carry me to the roof so high.

But I was far too big for the butterfly's wings,
and now he's tired, the poor little thing.

Meanwhile, the goose on the roof honked again;
he clearly wasn't trying to make any friends.

It was then at that moment that a dog walked by.
She thought she could talk to the goose and ask why.

So she barked and she barked, and it just got loud
because the noise never stopped, and there were two of them now!

**Through all of this wild and crazy commotion,
a flea volunteered with a fanciful notion.**

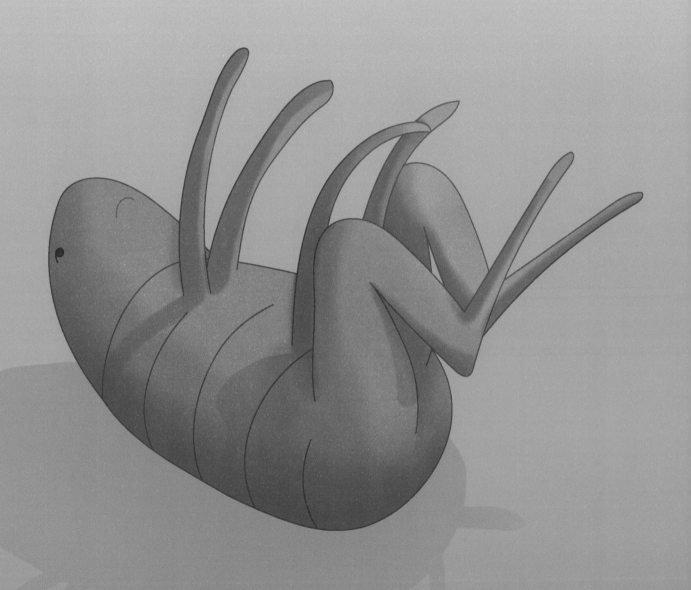

**But as soon as the flea began to jump all around,
he got lost and confused and landed upside down.**

The sun was about to set, and I was starting to worry.
Would anyone be able to help me in a hurry?

Because I still need to get up onto the roof,
and go find the flea and calm the dog's woofs.

And then rescue the cat who is getting upset
and go help a frog who I barely just met.

As I looked around at the scene, I sighed,
and saw the neighbor was watching, unsatisfied.

It was then that I noticed my dad had appeared
with a tall, silver ladder and not an ounce of fear.

He placed the ladder and locked it tight,
offered his hand and said it would be alright.

When we got to the top, I could finally see
what was causing the goose to honk and plea.

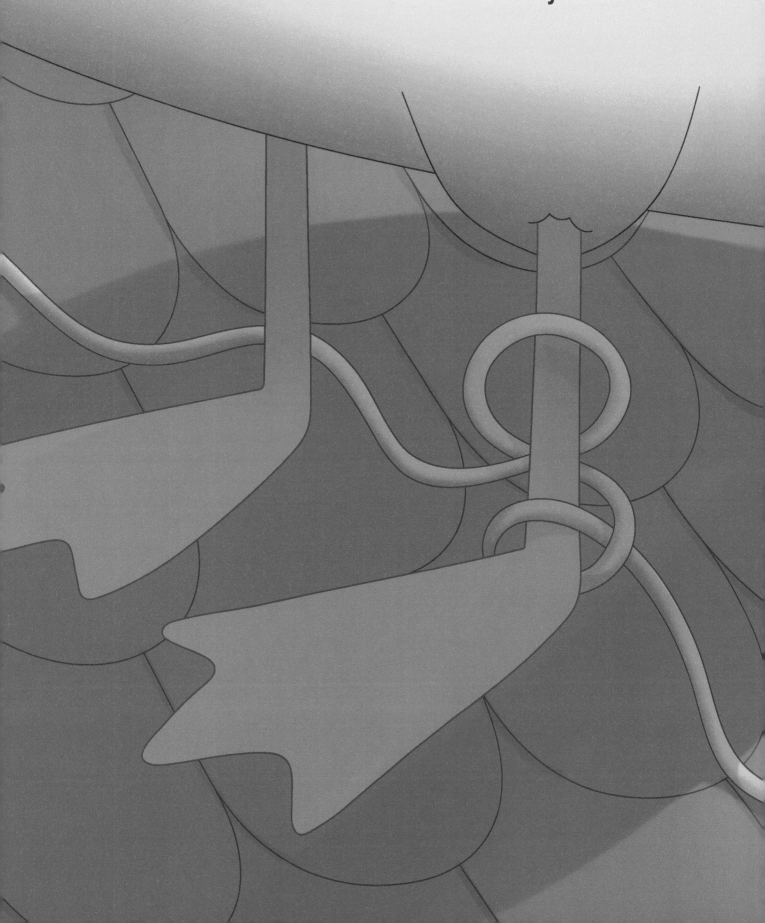

The goose's foot was stuck—oh my!
The bird was unable to leave or fly.

So I gently kneeled down and spoke quietly
as I loosened the string that was wrapped tightly.

Suddenly, he took off, soaring into the sky
and let out an echoey freedom cry.

I figured it was his way to say thanks,
for the goose on the roof was finally safe.

After climbing on down, we used that same ladder
to get the cat down before the cat got madder.

Then we walked to the street to stop all the cars,
so the frog could hop home to his log under the stars.

As we passed by the dog, my dad offered a treat,
and she was busy chewing her way down the street.

When the dog walked by, the flea picked up her scent
and followed her home and pitched a tent.

We found a place for the butterfly to rest
and sent flowers to apologize to the neighbor and his guests.

It's now so quiet, I almost miss the goose,
but I'm happy that he's no longer on my roof.

I am glad everyone is safe once again,
and I even managed to make a few friends.

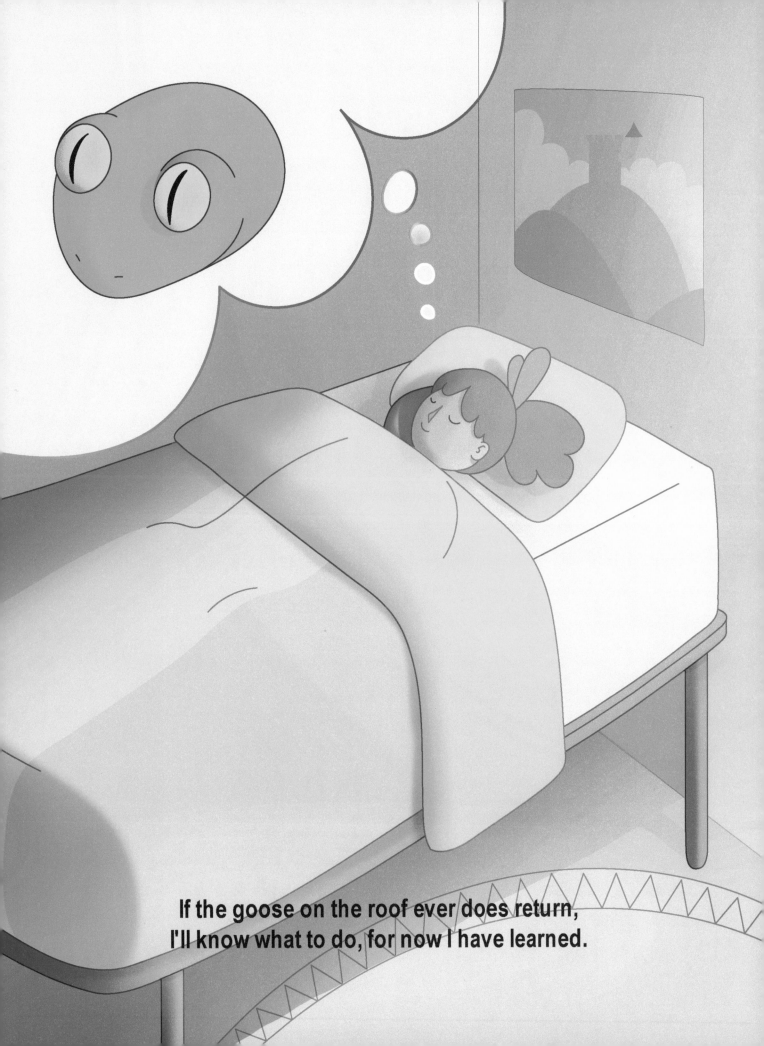

If the goose on the roof ever does return,
I'll know what to do, for now I have learned.

THE AUTHOR

Sarah Sommer enjoys working with words in a
way that makes the story feel musical and
rhythmical. She is a passionate animal
enthusiast and also enjoys the outdoors, trying
new cuisines, and playing her clarinet
and saxophone.
This is her first book.

THE ILLUSTRATOR

Born in an Italian city called Livorno, Martina spent
her childhood peeling her knees, falling down
from the bike and drawing a lot, encouraged by her
grandma who used to give her lots of crayons!
After she discovered a passion for comic books,
she decided to start her studies as an illustrator and
later to move to the UK where she improved her
skills with fine arts and digital techniques.

CPSIA information can be obtained
at www.ICGtesting.com
Printed in the USA
LVHW020952230520
656044LV00004B/158